Contents

Pedigree DreamWorks
ANIMATION SKG

Published by Pedigree Books Limited
Beech Hill House, Walnut Gardens, Exeter, Devon EX4 4DH
E-mail: books@pedigreegroup.co.uk
Published 2006
Over The Hedge TM & © 2006 DreamWorks Animation L.L.C.

Welcome to the Suburbs

£6.99

RJ

A charming small-time scavenger, RJ takes life – and everything else – as it comes. But when he takes a pile of food from a vicious bear, his carefree life is threatened. Can he make the haul of a lifetime and return the food before the bear wakes up?

Verne

Caring, selfless and hardworking, Verne is also neurotic and insecure. He wants to protect his 'family' at all costs and he just wants things to stay the same. But when cool RJ arrives, Verne's safe world starts to change!

the gang...

Hammy

Hammy has so much energy that it's tiring just watching him! He is full of excitement and has a way of innocently speaking the truth. He's not the brightest bulb in the pack, but he's sweet, charming and *very* fast!

Stella

Stella feels that nature dealt her a lousy hand. After all, her talent is that she stinks. Stella has no time for fools, but she's especially hard on herself.

...from over the hedge

Lou, Penny and the Kids

Penny and Lou are a rock-solid couple. Since the birth of the triplets, they have barely slept a wink; but they manage to keep smiling. Quillo, Bucky and Spike are hard work – but they're full of energy and fun!

Heather

When her father plays dead, Heather dies too – of embarrassment. To her, his act is pointless and humiliating. Will she ever appreciate her own inborn talent?

Ozzie

Ozzie takes the slightest threat as an opportunity to display his greatest talent – dying. Or, more accurately – 'playing possum'. He just wishes his chronically embarrassed teenage daughter would acknowledge her natural talent and embrace the family 'biz'.

MAKE YOUR OWN RUBBISH BIN PENCIL HOLDER

YOU WILL NEED:

- A grown up to help you
- An empty mini tube of crisps
- Thick black permanent marker
- Thick cardboard
- Tin foil
- Glue

WHAT TO DO:

1. Remove the lid from tube of crisps.

2. Ask a grown up to help you cut a length of tin foil that will fit around the outside of the tube.

3. Put a thin layer of glue around the outside of the tube, then stick the foil down carefully.

4. Draw thick black lines evenly down the sides of the tube. The lines should be 5mm apart.

5. Cut a piece of foil the same size as the top of the lid.

6. Put a thin layer of glue on the top of the lid and stick the foil to it.

7. Ask a grown up to help you cut out three cardboard strips, 6cm long and 1cm wide.

8. Cover the strips in foil, then make four folds in each strip to create handles. Stick one handle on each side of the bin and one on the lid.

STEP 3:

STEP 4:

STEP 8:

Now you have your own pencil holder, why not make some as presents for your friends?

THE END OF WINTER

RJ the raccoon dropped some coins into the vending machine.

A bag of crisps began to drop, but then they got stuck. RJ tried to reach the bag of crisps with a dinosaur grabber arm. He tried a boomerang. He even tried a golf club, but it was no use. The crisps were stuck – and RJ was *really* hungry.

He turned and looked over at the dark hillside. He could just see a dark opening – a cave. "Hmmm, Vincent," he said, thinking of the bear who lived in the cave. His tummy rumbled. What was he going to do?

Soon RJ was outside Vincent's cave. He peered inside. Somewhere in there, the big bear was fast asleep, hibernating. RJ could see a bag of crisps in the moonlight – it was even bigger than the one in the vending machine!
RJ decided to take the risk. He stepped very quietly towards the bag and picked it up. Then he saw another bag – and another! He picked all three up and then turned to leave. But just then he saw something that stopped him in his tracks…

It was a HUGE mountain of junk food! RJ had never seen so much! He piled all the junk food into a little red wagon, with a blue cooler on top. He was just about to leave when he saw something. A tube of Spuddies, his favourite crisps, was cuddled in Vincent's arms!
RJ couldn't resist. He slid the tube of Spuddies out of Vincent's arms and replaced it with a coffee cup. Then he backed away and opened the tube with a loud POP! Suddenly one big, yellow bear eyeball opened!

Vincent sat up and looked at RJ.
"Don't tell me you're dumb enough to actually try and steal my stuff?" he said. "RJ, I'm gonna have to kill you."
"I'm just a desperate guy trying to feed his family!" pleaded RJ, backing away.
"You don't *have* a family," said Vincent.
"OK, wait!" cried RJ. "Look, it's still in the cave. So technically, not stolen!"
But just then RJ bumped into the little red wagon.
It rolled out of the cave, down the hill to the road, where it was crushed by a speeding lorry!

RJ raced down the hill with Vincent at his heels. By the vending machines, Vincent caught him and opened his mouth wide.
"Wait!" yelled RJ. "I can get it all back!"
Vincent paused. "My red wagon?" he asked.
"Redder," RJ promised.
"The blue cooler?"
"On my list," RJ nodded.
"All right, RJ," said Vincent. "I'm going back to sleep. When that moon is full, I'm waking up. And *all* my stuff had better be right back where it was!"
"But that's just one week!" gasped RJ.
"Full moon, all my stuff," said Vincent. "And don't even think about running away. Because if you do, I will hunt you down and kill you."

In the forest, Verne the turtle was just waking up from his winter hibernation. He stepped out of the hollow log and looked out at the meadow. It was beautiful.

"Wow," said Verne happily. He turned back to the log and peered in at a pile of leaves. "Everybody! Wake up! Hibernation's over."

Hammy the squirrel shot out of the pile of leaves and darted past Verne.

"Oh, morning!" he said. "I gotta go wee-wee!"

"All right the rest of you. It's spring, that means we've gotta get to work!"

A skunk tail shot out of the pile. It was Stella!

"Ya'll better listen," she said. "I've been holding something in all winter and I'm about to let it out."

Very quickly five porcupines and two possums scattered.

"Thank you, Stella," said Verne.

The porcupine children, Quillo, Bucky and Spike, ran around their mum, Penny, in excitement.

"Good morning everyone!" cried Lou, their dad. "Just a super duper morning, eh?"

"Where's the food?" asked Hammy, talking at top speed as usual. "Is there any food left? I'm really hungry so is there any food left in here, huh?"

"We ate all the food, Hammy," said Heather. "During the winter. So we've gotta go and get some more now."

"Oh, right!" said Hammy. "I

buried some nuts in the woods and I know where they are and I'll be right back. Bye!"

He zipped away, knocking a clump of icy snow onto Ozzie the possum. "Whaaa!" cried Ozzie. He clutched his chest and dropped to the ground, his tongue dangling. Everyone looked at him and rolled their eyes. Heather forced a smile and turned to her father.

"Dad, it was just snow," she whispered, feeling very embarrassed.

"But it could have been a predator," said Ozzie.

Heather heaved a huge sigh and pulled Ozzie to his feet.

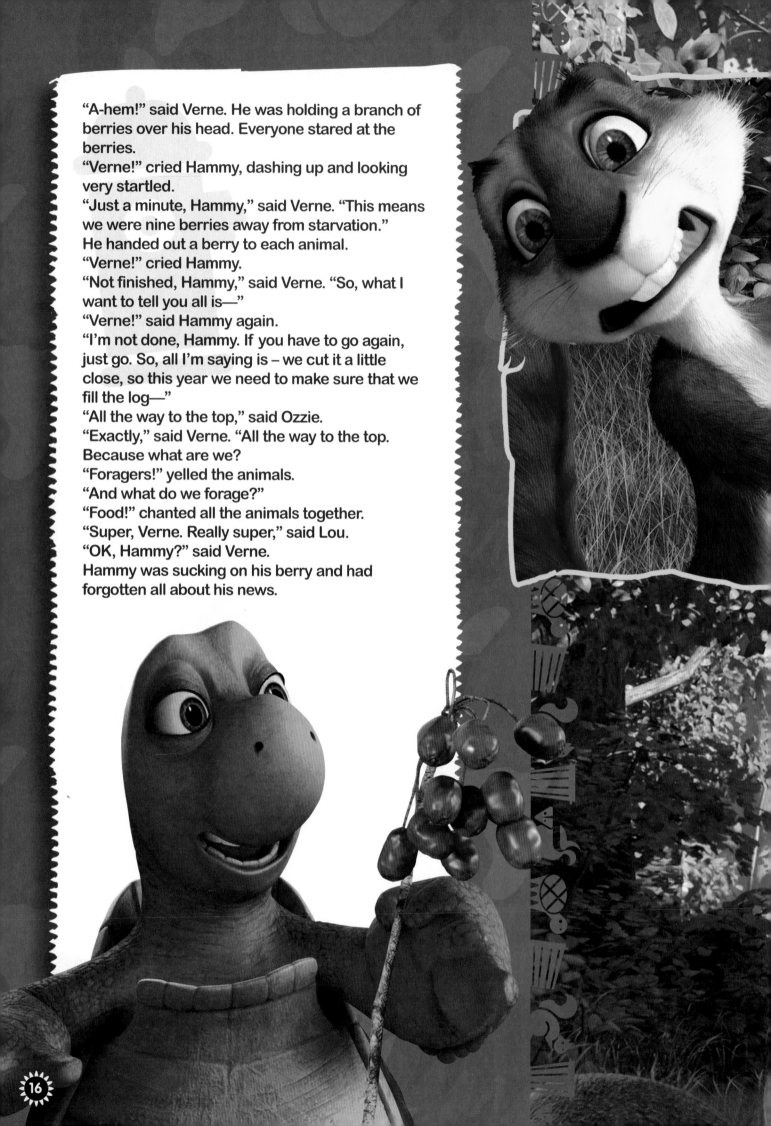

"A-hem!" said Verne. He was holding a branch of berries over his head. Everyone stared at the berries.

"Verne!" cried Hammy, dashing up and looking very startled.

"Just a minute, Hammy," said Verne. "This means we were nine berries away from starvation." He handed out a berry to each animal.

"Verne!" cried Hammy.

"Not finished, Hammy," said Verne. "So, what I want to tell you all is—"

"Verne!" said Hammy again.

"I'm not done, Hammy. If you have to go again, just go. So, all I'm saying is – we cut it a little close, so this year we need to make sure that we fill the log—"

"All the way to the top," said Ozzie.

"Exactly," said Verne. "All the way to the top. Because what are we?

"Foragers!" yelled the animals.

"And what do we forage?"

"Food!" chanted all the animals together.

"Super, Verne. Really super," said Lou.

"OK, Hammy?" said Verne.

Hammy was sucking on his berry and had forgotten all about his news.

"Hmm?" he said. "Oh! Oh! Oh! What was it, what was it, what was it, wait, right on the tip of my tongue… oh yeah! There's a weird thing over there I've never seen before. It's really scary! Follow me!" Hammy led them to the edge of the woods and pointed up.
It was a truly MASSIVE hedge. It stretched as far as their eyes could see.
"It never ends!" gasped Hammy.

Not far away, hidden behind a tree, RJ was watching the animals. He saw Verne step up to the hedge. All the animals followed him, huddled together.
"I'm scared!" said Spike.
"Shh, it's OK," said Penny. "It's just a… what is this thing, Lou?"
"I, well… it's a…" Lou stammered, "… it's… Verne?" Everyone looked at Verne.

"Well," said Verne. "It's, er, it's obviously some kind of… bush."
"I would be a lot less afraid of it if I just knew what it was called," said Penny.
"Let's call it Steve!" said Hammy. Verne stared at him.
"Steve?" Verne repeated.
"It's a pretty name," said Hammy.
"Steve sounds nice," Heather agreed.
"Yeah, I'm a lot less scared of Steve," Penny added.

"Oh great and powerful Steve!" cried Ozzie, looking up at the hedge. "What do you want?"
Just then, a woman on the other side of the hedge called out to her son. "You get over here right now!" she yelled. The animals leapt into a tight huddle. They thought it was Steve who had spoken!

Hammy walked towards the hedge.
"Hammy, get back here!" yelled Verne.
"But Steve is angry," said Hammy.
"I think it came from the other side of Steve – I mean the bush – I mean… geez!" cried Verne. "Look, there's only one way we're gonna find out what this thing is and what this is all about. I'm gonna go check it out."

He drew on all his courage and stepped up to the hedge.
Just then he tripped and fell into the hedge!
"Steve ate Verne!" Ozzie screamed.
Stella pounded up to the hedge.
"All right, Steve!" she yelled. "You brought this on yourself!"
She turned around and pointed her dangerous end at the hedge.
From inside the hedge, Verne reached out to her.
"Stella, don't!" he cried. "I'm not eaten, I just tripped. I'm gonna go over there. Just don't anybody move."
He disappeared back into the hedge.

Behind the animals, RJ climbed the tree to carry on watching Verne.

Verne crept through the hedge and stared in amazement at the sight that met his eyes. None of this had been here when he went into hibernation! Where were all the oak trees? Where were all the berry bushes?

"What is this place?" he asked himself. He looked around at a perfect lawn. He didn't know that he was in the middle of a perfectly manicured garden. Suddenly, a dragonfly fluttered into an insect zapper and got fried. Verne gulped. This new place seemed dangerous! Verne walked away and tripped over a turtle-shaped stepping stone. Then a frog-shaped sprinkler sprayed him in the face. Verne backed away into a stone column. A reflector ball rolled off the column and chased him! He managed to jump on top of it and tried to balance as it rolled along. As he crashed into a barbeque, a collection of barbeque utensils rained down on him.

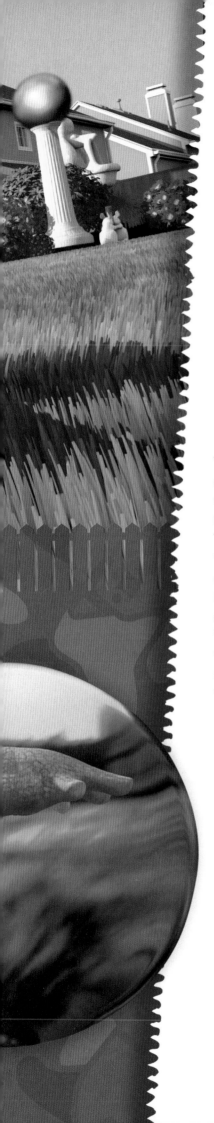

Verne pulled his limbs inside his shell, just missing getting sliced! One of the barbeque knives cut the hose and water spewed out. The hose whipped around like a snake. It sent Verne flying over the fence and SMACK BANG onto a toy car!

The car rolled down the driveway – straight into the path of a real 4x4! "Ahhhh!" yelled Verne as the tiny car rolled under the big car, shot out at the other side and hit the mailbox post. Before Verne could catch his breath, two bikes whizzed past, flipping him into the middle of the street and spinning him in circles.

When Verne stopped spinning he saw a hockey puck slide right up to the opening of his shell, followed by three roller-hockey players, who skated up to Verne. They slap-shot him over a fence – and back through the hedge!

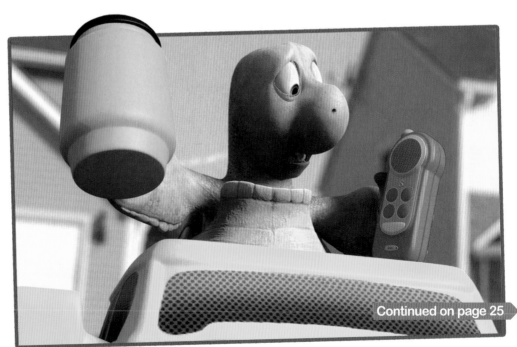

Continued on page 25

VERNE'S DOOR HANGER

Sometimes you just want some privacy in your own shell. This awesome door hanger will tell your family whether they can disturb you or not!

COME IN!

KEEP OUT!

1 Trace or copy the design opposite onto a piece of white card.

2 Trim the card to the right shape.

3 Trace the other side of the hanger onto the other side of the card.

4 Colour it in!

5 Hang over your bedroom doorknob to show whether you want visitors or not.

You can use this design to make cool door hangers for all your friends and family!

spot the difference!

These two snaps of the gang look just the same, but there are 6 differences between them! Grab a pen and circle all six differences.

RJ's Expedition

WHOOSH! Verne came bursting through the hedge, hit the ground and let out a huge gasp. His friends raced over to him.

"Verne!" cried Quillo.

"Jeepers!" Penny gasped.

"Are you OK?" asked Heather.

"What was over there?" Ozzie added.

"Freaky, pink primates," panted Verne. "They must have come while we were hibernating. And they… it was awful… they had wheels on their feet and they had these sticks and they were whacking me with these sticks like it was some sort of sick game."

"You should have died!" said Ozzie. "You should have laid down and died!"

"Dad…" Heather groaned.

Up in the tree, RJ shook his head.

"That's not the worst part," Verne went on. "Half the forest is gone. Oh… the oak trees and the berry bushes, they're just… they're just… gone." The animals were stunned into silence.

"What'll we do for food?" asked Stella at last.

"I don't know," said Verne. "But here's what I do know… we will be fine – as long as no one goes over Steve again."

RJ decided that it was time to show himself. He walked down a branch towards the animals.
"I'm RJ," he said. "Now, please don't think I'm prying, but I couldn't help overhearing, and I think I can shed a little light on what this whole hedge situation is about."

He came to join them. "You're hibernators, right?" he asked. "You gather up a bunch of food, store it away for the winter?"
"Uh-huh," said Hammy. "We fill the log."
"Let me ask you," RJ said. "How long does it take? You know, to fill the log?"
"274 days," Heather replied.
"Oh!" said RJ. "Ever done it in a week?"
"A week?" chuckled Verne. "That's impossible."
"Not if we work together!" said RJ. "You've got the food gathering skills, I've got the know-how and they have the food."

"How much food?" Heather asked.

"Loads of food," said RJ. "Heaps of food. Food out the wazoo!"

Verne stepped in front of the others.

"I really don't think we're interested in eating whatever kind of food comes out of a wazoo."

"I don't know," said Lou. "The guy's making a lot of sense to me. I think we should listen."

"Yeah, I'm OK with wazoo food there," Penny agreed.

"No you're not," said Verne. "The tail is tingling."

All the animals began to panic. RJ was confused.

"Hold on, hold on," he said. "The what is what?"

"When something doesn't feel right, my tail tingles," Verne explained.

"This isn't something you need to be afraid of," said RJ.

"Whatever," said Verne. "Thanks for stopping by – we're not interested."

"Not interested in the most delicious food you've ever tasted?" RJ said. "Come on—"

"NO!" Verne repeated. "Not interested!"

RJ had an idea. He pulled a bag of crisps from his bag and let the animals smell it.

"What is that?" cried Hammy in ecstasy.

RJ handed out the crisps and the animals devoured them. They couldn't get enough!

"Those were good!" Stella cried.

"It's all good and we're going over there... tonight!" RJ grinned.

RJ took the animals through the hedge and introduced them to suburbia. Lawn sprinklers spurted into life. RJ swished his tail across a motion sensor and lights clicked on, lighting up the garden. The animals gasped. They had never seen anything like it! It was beautiful!
"How's that tail?" RJ asked Verne.
"Listen," said Verne. "If anybody in this family gets hurt, I'm holding you personally responsible."
"They're having a good time," said RJ. "I'll take responsibility for that."

Just then the front door of the house opened and a woman walked out, talking on her mobile phone. Her name was Gladys.
"What is that?" gasped the animals.
"Easy, easy, don't worry," said RJ. "That's just a human being. And they are just as scared of us as we are of them."

Gladys reached into the 4x4 and pulled out a box full of shopping. Then she slammed the door and went back into the house.

"Could we just get the food and go?" asked Verne. "Really, do they have it or not?"

"Didn't you see it?" RJ chuckled. "It was in the box. They've always got food with them. We eat to live, these guys live to eat. Let me show you what I'm talking about."

RJ led the animals around the outside of the house, peering in through windows. They saw a woman ordering food on the phone. They saw a man delivering pizza to the front door.

"That is the portal for the passing of the food," RJ told them. "Humans bring the food, take the food, ship the food. They drive the food. They wear the food."

RJ showed them a barbeque for getting the food hot – and a cooler for keeping it cold. He showed them a family sitting at the dinner table and praying.

"That is the altar where they worship food," said RJ.

All the human beings RJ showed the animals were doing something that involved food. One woman was exercising so that she could eat more food. A man was using a steak to heal a black eye and a woman was using cucumber slices to soothe her eyes. They saw a fast food restaurant in the distance.

RJ held up his arms.
"So, you think they have enough?" he asked. "Well, they don't. They have too much! And what do they do with the stuff they don't eat? They put it in gleaming, silver cans – just for us."
He kicked over a few rubbish bins. Food spilled out.
"Sweet jeepers!" cried Penny.
"Dig in!" RJ told them.
The hungry animals dived into the heap of crusts and bones and greasy paper towels. All Verne could do was watch as his friends gorged themselves.

Just then, a fat Persian cat stepped through a cat flap and saw them!
"Halt!" said the cat. "Intruders! Intruders! Get out, all of you!"
The back door flew open and Gladys appeared with a broom. She attacked them, only just missing Hammy!
"To the hedge!" RJ shouted.

Back behind the hedge, the animals tried to catch their breath.
"See what I mean?" Verne exclaimed. "That's what I was talking about! These humans don't want us around!"
"Come on, think about the food," said RJ. "It was worth it for that food, huh? That stuff is to die for!"
The animals gasped in horror.
"Let me rephrase that—" said RJ quickly. But Verne stopped him.
"No, 'to die for' – you nailed that part," he said. "Look, maybe our little forest life looks primitive. But gee, I think I speak for the whole family when I say – we want nothing to do with anything that's over that hedge."
Verne turned to walk away. One by one, the other animals followed him. RJ pleaded with them, but they had made up their minds. They never wanted to go over the hedge again.

That night, RJ didn't sleep very well. He had a nightmare about Vincent – and what he would do if he didn't get his food back. RJ had to think of a plan...

Next morning, the animals started to gather their food for the winter, just as usual. But this time they weren't enjoying it at all. They kept thinking about RJ and the delicious things he had shown them over the hedge.

Verne was carrying an armful of grass and bark over to the hollow log when RJ appeared. All the animals were delighted to see him – except Verne.
"What are you doing here?" he scowled.
"I'm here to help you with your foraging thing," said RJ. "Look, Verne, you said a word yesterday about your little gang here, starts with an 'F'. Do you remember what it was?"
"Family?" said Verne.
"Right, right, that," RJ said. "You know, that got me right here." He pointed to his heart.

All the animals felt sorry for RJ. They wanted him to stay, but Verne did not look as if he were going to change his mind. Everyone stared at Verne with pleading eyes.
"All right, all right!" said Verne at last. "Hey, er, RJ? You can… you can stay."
"I knew beneath this hard crispy outside there was a soft nougaty centre in there!" RJ cried.
"Do you mind if I call you Uncle Verne?"
"With every bone in my body," Verne replied.

"Great!" said RJ, who wasn't listening to a word. "Hey, can I work with Hammy?"

RJ put one arm around Hammy's shoulders and led him away until they were out of sight of the others. Then he held out a cookie. The squirrel smelt it and his eyes grew very wide.
"You like this cookie?" asked RJ. "Well, I know where we can get some cookies so valuable that they are hand delivered by uniformed officers."
"I'd like a cookie!" said Hammy.

Continued on page 38

Who's Over Your Hedge?

Create your very own adventures for RJ, Verne and the gang!

What to do:

1. Trace or photocopy these pictures onto paper and then stick them onto thick card.

2. Colour them in! Try to match the colours to the characters in the book using your pens and pencils.

3. Cut out the support tabs. Cut along the dotted lines and assemble as shown in the diagram to the right so they can stand up by themselves.

MASSIVE MUNCHING MAZE

RJ and his friends are on a raid. Each friend is trying to find the most items of delicious food to store in the hollow log!

Follow the coloured lines with your finger and count up how many items of food each animal has collected. Write the numbers in the boxes at the bottom of the page. Who has found the most food?

Animal Heists

Two Trail Guide Gals were pulling a squeaky red wagon down the pavement. It was filled with cookies. RJ and Hammy watched from a tree. Hammy's eyes opened very wide.

"And there they are… America's most coveted cookies. Love Handles, Skinny Mints, Neener Neeners and Smackeroons. And guess what? They're all yours!" Hammy started to move forward, but RJ stopped him.

"But you just said they're mine," said Hammy with tears in his eyes.

"They will be," said RJ, "if we successfully marry your manic energy to my brilliant plan! You with me, kid?"

Hammy agreed and RJ explained his plan. They were going to scare the girls and make them run away – leaving the cookies behind!

"Now, listen up kid," RJ said. "What we're going for here is vicious, man-eating, rabid squirrel. Can you handle that?"

Hammy nodded and RJ got to work. He messed up Hammy's fur and sprayed whipped cream around his mouth so it looked like foam.

With a howling screech, Hammy hopped madly towards the two girl scouts.

"YAR, AR, RAA, RAA, I'm rabid!" Hammy shouted. "I'm foaming at the mouth! I want my cookies"

But one of the girls bashed Hammy over the head with her Trail Guide Gals Manual and sprayed him with mace! Hammy yelled and screamed.

Verne ran through the hedge. He had been searching for Hammy everywhere!

"What is going on?" he demanded.

"Everything's under control," said RJ. "Just go back to the hedge."

"You call that under control?" Verne yelled. "He's under attack!"

Verne rushed into the road, but he was sucked up by a street sweeper! The sweeper spat him out and he bounced on the road and popped right out of his shell! He landed on one of the girls' faces – completely naked!

The girls ran away, screaming. RJ grabbed the little red wagon and led Hammy back towards the hedge. Verne was about to follow when he heard something very scary. Gladys had overheard the girls and was making a call on her mobile phone.

"Do you carry animal traps?" she said.

When Verne got back home, he found the animals all gorging on the cookies. RJ was delighted – he had got a new red wagon for Vincent!

"Oh jeepers, that is good!" said Penny. "Anything that tastes this good has to be good for you."

"This is amazing," said Heather.

"Come on, dig in," said RJ. "Because this, my friends, is just the beginning."

But Verne felt worried.

Over the next few days, RJ led the animals on a massive raid. Verne was the only one who wouldn't help. He just kept gathering weeds and berries. Thanks to the others, the log was filling up with junk food very fast. And, secretly, RJ was ticking items off his list.

Meanwhile, Gladys had noticed the rubbish bins scattered all over the place and the paw prints on her car. She had called an exterminator.

As the animals were celebrating, RJ heard a car. He peered through the hedge and saw a blue cooler on the roof rack – exactly like Vincent's. It was just what he needed! He whistled for everyone to follow him.

As the others followed RJ, Verne walked up to the log and saw that it was full. Then he heard a car screech to a halt and Ozzie cry out in pain. "Ozzie!" yelled Verne.

Verne rushed through the hedge and into the road. A crowd of humans was gathering around Ozzie, who was lying on the pavement. It looked as if he had been hit by the car!

Behind the humans, RJ was leading the animals up to the roof of the car. A little boy moved towards the car and Ozzie opened one eye. He was just acting!

Ozzie had to keep the humans away from the car! He twitched and the little boy hurried back to the others. Ozzie launched into a death scene – his favourite thing! The humans could not take their eyes off him. He squeaked and staggered around in circles. It was the performance of a lifetime!

Behind the humans, the other animals freed the cooler from its cords and pushed it towards the back of the roof. Verne called up to them.
"I'm telling you, you went too far this time!" he said. "Let's just get out of here and leave this—"
He was interrupted when his friends pushed the cooler off the top of the car – and it landed on top of him!
"Nice catch, Verne," said RJ as Ozzie finished his death scene.
"Everybody get out of here right now!" Verne yelled.

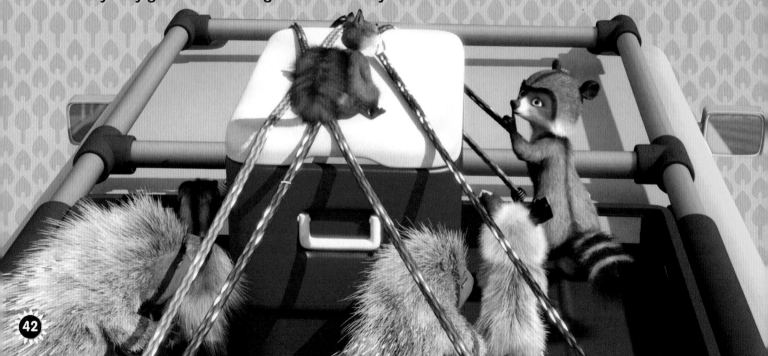

RJ and the other animals dragged the heavy cooler towards the hedge. But just then, Verne felt the ground rumble. He peered out from under the car and saw an exterminator van drive up to the scene. A man stepped out and walked up to Gladys.
"I believe someone phoned about an animal problem?" he said. "The solution is standing before you. Dwayne La Fontaine is here."
"Where have you been?" hissed Gladys. "I'm throwing a 'Welcome to the Neighbourhood' party tomorrow and so far Debbie's car has killed more animals than you have."
"Stand down, sister," said Dwayne. "I personally guarantee that there will not be a living thing at this party."

He leaned towards Ozzie and sniffed. He guessed that Ozzie was faking! Ozzie opened one eye and saw that RJ and the others were almost at the fence. Dwayne grabbed a claw-like tool from his belt – but Ozzie leapt up and sprinted towards the hedge! "You were a great audience!" he chuckled.

When Verne got back to the clearing, RJ and the other animals were having a full-blown celebration. They couldn't believe that they had actually done it! They had found it so exciting!

Verne could not believe that they were celebrating. Hadn't they seen the danger? Everyone was congratulating Ozzie on his performance. Even Heather was impressed!

"But let's not forget our brilliant leadership – RJ!" Ozzie cried. All the animals clapped, hooted and hollered, patting RJ on the back. Verne could hardly believe his eyes.

But later, RJ was starting to feel guilty about how he was tricking the others.

"Whoa," he said to himself, walking towards the log. "RJ, what are you doing, man? You are getting in way too deep. Just get the food, feed the bear. Get the food, feed the bear."

Then he gave a huge gasp. The log was empty! The food – the wagon – the crisps – they had all gone!

RJ popped his head through the hedge. He saw Verne pulling the red wagon into a garden. He had piled all the food into it!

RJ ran over and grabbed the back of the wagon. "What are you doing?" he yelled.

""I'm getting things back to the way they were," said Verne.

"No, don't," said RJ. "How about I just leave?"

"Good," Verne agreed. "You leave and I return this stuff to the rightful owners.

"What?" asked RJ. "Why?"

"Because we've angered the humans," said Verne.

Verne and RJ started a tug of war with the wagon. Then suddenly RJ realised something awful. They were right next to a kennel – and there was a huge dog asleep inside it!

"Verne," whispered RJ. "Move slow, keep your voice low and follow me."

But Verne hadn't seen the dog. He thought this was another of RJ's tricks!

"No," he said. "I'm not falling for any more of your smooth talk! I don't know what you're up to but my entire shell is tingling. And you know what, I'm listening to it this time and I'm putting my foot down!"

He stamped his foot down onto a rubber toy dog. It squeaked!

The dog woke up straight away. It thought Verne was something to play with! RJ dived out of the way as the dog snatched Verne up in its mouth and shook him!

RJ tried to get away but the dog spotted him and a great chase began all around the garden! It was pandemonium! The dog crashed into a barbeque and a patio set. Almost all the food in the wagon was destroyed as Verne and RJ tried to escape. A gas canister from the barbeque got attached to the wagon. So did the patio-set umbrella! Then the gas canister ignited and sent Verne and RJ shooting up a slide and into the air!

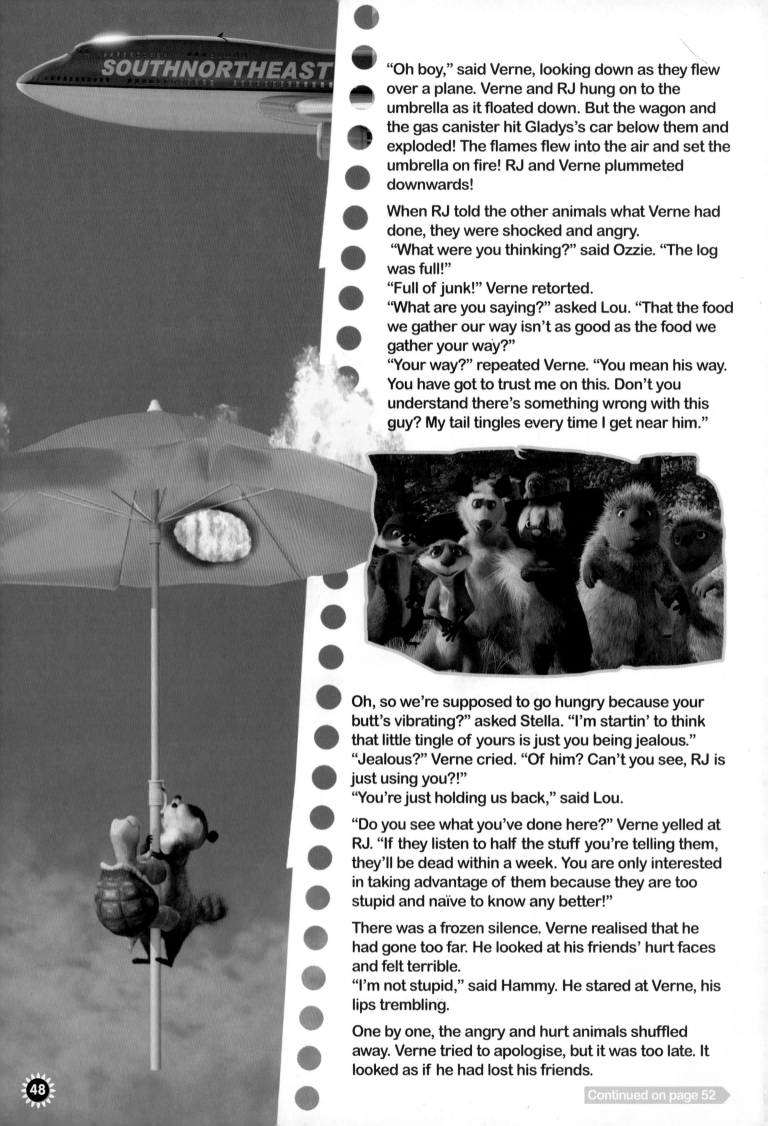

"Oh boy," said Verne, looking down as they flew over a plane. Verne and RJ hung on to the umbrella as it floated down. But the wagon and the gas canister hit Gladys's car below them and exploded! The flames flew into the air and set the umbrella on fire! RJ and Verne plummeted downwards!

When RJ told the other animals what Verne had done, they were shocked and angry.
"What were you thinking?" said Ozzie. "The log was full!"
"Full of junk!" Verne retorted.
"What are you saying?" asked Lou. "That the food we gather our way isn't as good as the food we gather your way?"
"Your way?" repeated Verne. "You mean his way. You have got to trust me on this. Don't you understand there's something wrong with this guy? My tail tingles every time I get near him."

Oh, so we're supposed to go hungry because your butt's vibrating?" asked Stella. "I'm startin' to think that little tingle of yours is just you being jealous."
"Jealous?" Verne cried. "Of him? Can't you see, RJ is just using you?!"
"You're just holding us back," said Lou.

"Do you see what you've done here?" Verne yelled at RJ. "If they listen to half the stuff you're telling them, they'll be dead within a week. You are only interested in taking advantage of them because they are too stupid and naïve to know any better!"

There was a frozen silence. Verne realised that he had gone too far. He looked at his friends' hurt faces and felt terrible.
"I'm not stupid," said Hammy. He stared at Verne, his lips trembling.

One by one, the angry and hurt animals shuffled away. Verne tried to apologise, but it was too late. It looked as if he had lost his friends.

Continued on page 52

Ozzie's Wordsearch

This is a puzzle to die for! Here are the names of some of my friends – and my enemies! Can you find them all in the grid?

- Vincent ✓
- Gladys ✓
- Verne ✓
- Stella ✓
- Penny ✓
- Heather ✓
- Hammy

V	F	W	E	R	L	Y	K	I	O
I	H	J	K	P	E	N	N	Y	L
N	G	H	F	D	S	D	A	L	G
C	M	A	B	V	S	C	Z	A	S
E	N	M	Q	W	G	E	R	S	T
N	L	M	P	O	L	I	U	T	Y
T	K	Y	H	E	A	T	H	E	R
J	H	G	F	D	D	S	A	L	A
P	N	M	B	V	Y	C	X	L	S
V	E	R	N	E	S	Y	U	A	I

Make an Over The Hedge PIZZA!

Roll up your sleeves and get busy in the kitchen. You're gonna make the yummiest, scrummiest pizza any animal could wish for! RJ, Verne and Hammy will want to share this pizza with you!

You will need:

1 ready-made pizza base

Tomato paste pizza sauce

Your favourite fruit, vegetables, cheese and meat

Preparation

Clean your hands

Put on your apron

Ask a grown up to preheat the oven to about 180 degrees.

Spread a thick layer of tomato paste all over your pizza base. Then use some thin strips of cheese to divide the pizza into quarters.

Making the Pizza

Use the ingredients below to add layers to each quarter and make a delicious slice of pizza for each of you!

1. RJ's Quarter

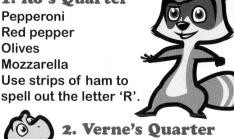

Pepperoni
Red pepper
Olives
Mozzarella
Use strips of ham to spell out the letter 'R'.

2. Verne's Quarter

Spinach
Asparagus
Pineapple
Ricotta
Use some green pepper to spell out the letter 'V'.

3. Hammy's Quarter

Mushrooms
Broccoli
Grapes
Parmesan
Use some pineapple to spell out the letter 'H'.

4. Your Quarter!

Now you can really let your taste buds go wild! Pick all the things you like best from the lists to create a custom-made pizza slice – just for you!

Pick your vegetables
Mushrooms
Onions
Pepper
Spinach
Broccoli
Asparagus

Pick your fruit
Tomatoes
Pineapple
Grapes
Raisins
Apples

Pick your meat
Pepperoni
Ham
Chicken
Sausage

Pick your extras
Green chillis
Olives
Sweetcorn
Anchovies

Pick your cheese
Mozzarella
Cheddar
Ricotta
Parmesan

Use some food to spell out the first letter of your name!

Cooking the Pizza!

Now you've finished designing your perfect pizza, it's time to put it in the oven!

Put your pizza on an oven tray sprayed with olive oil, so that the pizza doesn't stick.
Ask an adult to help you put the pizza into the oven.
After about 15–25 minutes, ask an adult to help you take the pizza out of the oven. The cheese should be a golden brown, but it should not be burnt.
Use a pizza slicer to divide the pizza into quarters. You might want to share the quarters with your friends. Or you might want to keep it all to yourself, it tastes so good!

Now you know how to make a pizza, you can try designing lots of different ones! Make a pizza for your best friend, using all their favourite things! Or you could use the food to make a face on your pizza! Have fun!

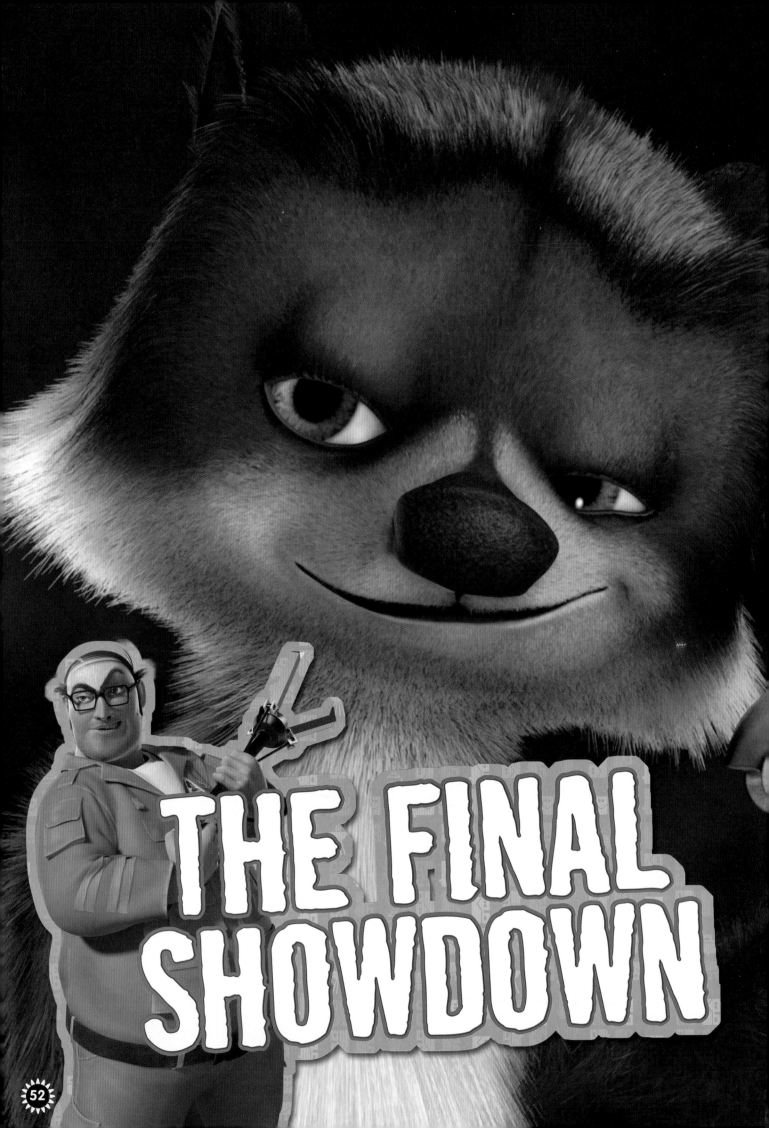

THE FINAL SHOWDOWN

Verne spent a long time thinking about his behaviour. At last he knew what he had to do.

Meanwhile, RJ was watching Gladys and Dwayne through the hedge. Dwayne was testing all the traps he had set to catch and kill the animals! "And did you put this one in?" asked Gladys. "This 'De-peltor Turbo'?"

Dwayne showed her what the trap could do. He tossed a little stuffed rabbit into the garden, where it crossed a laser beam. BANG! The rabbit was blasted into a metal cage. "What have I done?" said RJ.

Just then, Verne came up to RJ. He told RJ that he was sorry he had taken the food. Then RJ spotted the food arriving for Gladys's party.
"You know what," said RJ, thinking fast. "I know a place that is so chalked full of food, we could get it all back in one night."
"Great," said Verne. "Let's go!"

But first there was something Verne had to do. He went to find his friends.
"I'm sorry," he said.
The animals looked at each other. Then they all piled onto Verne and gave him a huge hug. They forgave him.

"Now, the plan works in three simple steps," RJ said. "Step one, kill the lights. Step two, get inside. Step three, get out with mountain of food."
"But this place is like a fortress," said Ozzie. "Walls, so high. Doors, impenetrable. How will we get in?"
RJ reminded them of the cat with the electronic collar. The collar worked like a key.
"You think he's just gonna hand over his collar to you?" Stella asked.
"Not to me, my femme fatale," said RJ. "To you."

That night, RJ gave Stella a complete makeover. He hid her white stripe and made her look stunning! She was transformed into a gorgeous black cat. RJ looked up at the night sky. The moon was full. Vincent would be waking up in the morning.

RJ launched a fishing hook and line through the air. The hook landed on the roof of Gladys's house, catching in the gutter. Hammy set off down the fishing line. At last he reached the roof and kicked the line back to RJ. He jumped down the drain and onto the lawn, then went to the De-peltor Turbo trap control switch and turned it off. He had disabled the lasers! RJ gave the thumbs-up sign to Verne.

"I thought we'd be dead by step two, so this is going great," said Verne.

The red wagon flew into the garden with everyone in it. Now it was Stella's turn! She walked up to the house and into the light from the porch.
The Persian cat, Tiger, walked out of the cat flap.
"Who goes there?" he asked.
Stella struck a pose and began to charm Tiger. While he was looking into her eyes, the others scooted across the garden and arrived at the back door. Stella took off Tiger's collar and threw it to her friends. Verne put it around his wrist and it opened the cat flap!

The animals crept in through the cat flap. RJ slid over to the fridge and opened it. The animals gasped when they saw all the food.
Penny and Lou hit the fridge and started to clean it out. Ozzie and Heather went to clear the shelves in the cabinets and the pantry. The animals made a chain and passed the food down it to Hammy, who zipped in and out of the cat flap, loading the wagon.

Outside, Stella was keeping Tiger's attention away from her friends. Suddenly the coffee maker went off. Gladys was coming down the stairs!

"Get down and stay down!" cried Verne. "Move. Move!"

The animals hid all around the kitchen as Gladys walked in, yawning. She got her coffee and opened a high cupboard door. RJ saw the Spuddies in the cupboard!

Gladys started to walk back upstairs.

"C'mon!" said Verne. "We've gotta go before she comes back!"

"No!" RJ replied. "Not without those Spuddies!"

He ran towards the cupboard, ordering Heather to watch Gladys.

"I'm on it, RJ!" said Heather, running upstairs.

"No, Heather!" cried Ozzie. "Wait!"

RJ started to climb towards the cupboard.

"RJ, the wagon's full!" cried Verne. "Let's get out of here!"

"Hang on, Vincent, this'll only take a second."

"Vincent?" repeated Verne, climbing up after him.

"Where?" cried RJ in terror.

"Who's Vincent?" asked Verne.

"Oh, Verne, Vincent – simple slip of the bear – tongue!" RJ stammered. "Er, just bear with me is what I meant to say, heh-heh. There's no bear."

Verne's tail went into mega-tingle mode.

Meanwhile, Heather was climbing the stairs. But as she reached the top, Gladys turned and saw her! Gladys kicked Heather and she was thrown down the stairs. She landed – dead still!

"Heather!" cried Ozzie.

Gladys ran to the bedroom phone to call Dwayne.

"Heather," Ozzie moaned as he rushed to her side. Heather opened her eyes.

"I thought you were dead," Ozzie said.

"I learned from the best, Dad," said Heather, as Ozzie pulled her to her feet.

"That's my girl," he said, with tears of relief in his eyes.

In the kitchen, RJ was still trying to reach the Spuddies.

"What's going on, RJ?" Verne asked.

"Nothing!" RJ replied.

"Well then, let's get out of here because we have what we need."

"Hey listen!" cried RJ. "I've got about this long to hand over that wagon load of food to a homicidal bear, and if these Spuddies aren't on the menu then I will be!"

"What?" yelled Verne. The animals gasped in shock. RJ and Verne struggled and the Spuddies flew everywhere! Gladys ran into the kitchen and screamed when she saw the animals and the mess.

RJ steered the wagon of food down the hill towards Dwayne's van. The wagon hit the van and RJ landed on the bonnet. Dwayne slammed on the brakes and all the cages slid to the front of the van. They smacked Dwayne in the back of the head and knocked him out!

Stella heard the scream and ran in through the cat flap, brushing off her disguise. RJ quickly ran out of the cat flap. As the animals ran towards the cat flap, Gladys blocked their way out! They ran the other way, but Dwayne appeared, with a net gun! Soon he had netted them all. They were prisoners! Dwayne put the animals into cages and took them out to his van.

RJ was taking the wagon up the hill to Vincent's cave. But he met Vincent on the way! Vincent was impressed that RJ had used his friends and left them to be captured. But when RJ turned and saw his friends in trouble, he was horrified. He grabbed the wagon, leapt on it and rode it down the hill!

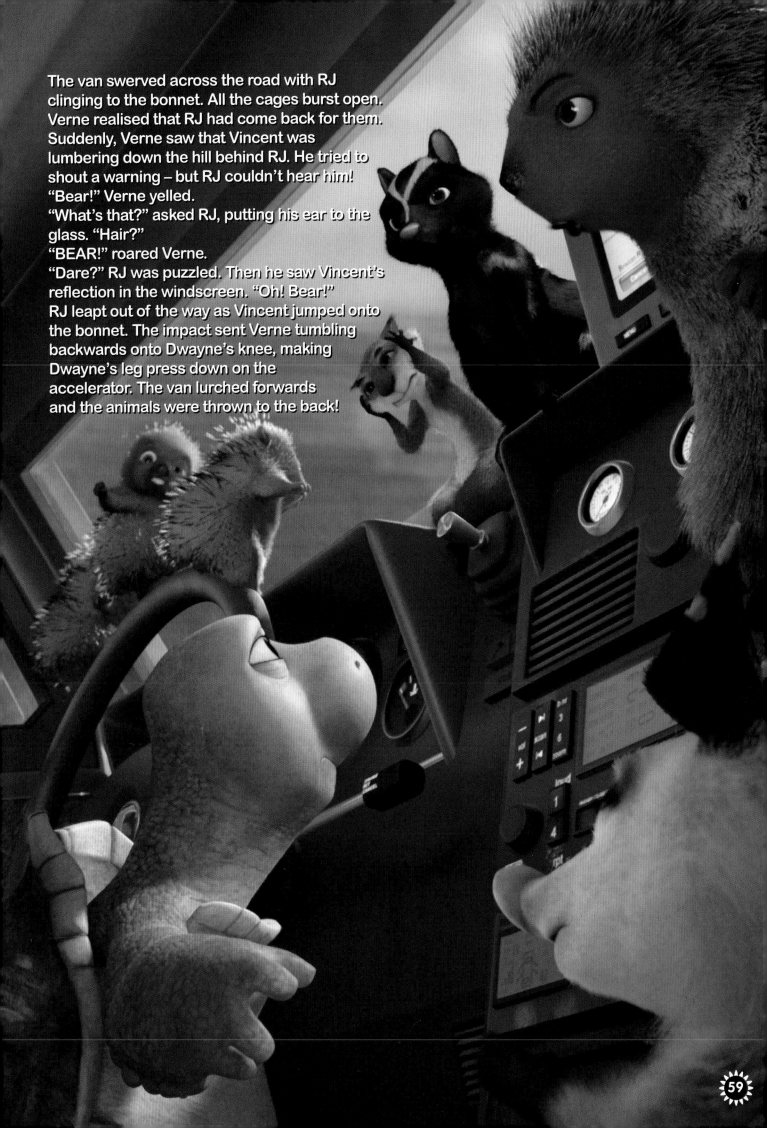

The van swerved across the road with RJ clinging to the bonnet. All the cages burst open. Verne realised that RJ had come back for them. Suddenly, Verne saw that Vincent was lumbering down the hill behind RJ. He tried to shout a warning – but RJ couldn't hear him!

"Bear!" Verne yelled.

"What's that?" asked RJ, putting his ear to the glass. "Hair?"

"BEAR!" roared Verne.

"Dare?" RJ was puzzled. Then he saw Vincent's reflection in the windscreen. "Oh! Bear!"

RJ leapt out of the way as Vincent jumped onto the bonnet. The impact sent Verne tumbling backwards onto Dwayne's knee, making Dwayne's leg press down on the accelerator. The van lurched forwards and the animals were thrown to the back!

Vincent chased RJ all over the van as it sped along. The porcupine kids grabbed the wheel and tried to shake the bear off the van, but Vincent and RJ were both clinging on.

"Let me in! Let me in!" RJ pleaded. At first the animals didn't want to save RJ, but Verne knew that the raccoon was trying to help!

"But Verne, you're the one who always says trust your tail!" bellowed Lou.

"But it's not tingling," said Verne.

Ozzie let RJ in as the porcupine kids steered the van towards a big balloon display. Vincent was caught up in the balloons and pulled high into the sky! The animals cheered and whooped!

The van crash landed in Gladys's house and the animals clambered out and sped back to the hedge. But Vincent had landed in a tree and he was waiting for them! He gave a loud ROAR!

The friends hurtled back through the hedge into Gladys's garden, where Dwayne was waiting. He jabbed at them with a cattle prod. They were trapped between the bear and the humans!

RJ and Verne tricked Vincent into throwing himself at the humans. Meanwhile, Hammy drank some cola which gave him the speed to turn on the De-peltor Turbo without the humans seeing him. Then Dwayne, Gladys and Vincent set off the lasers. The De-peltor Turbo came to life!

After an enormous explosion, the De-peltor Turbo stopped. Dwayne, Vincent and Gladys were caught!

In the clearing, the animals celebrated their victory, even Tiger the cat. All except RJ. He was watching from the sidelines. Verne turned to him. "You know, RJ," he said. "Just for the record, if you had told us that all that food you were trying to get was to pay back an angry bear, we would've given it to you. That's what families do – they look out for each other." "I've never really had anything like that," said RJ.
"So, what do ya say?" said Verne. "You wanna be a part of it?"

RJ accepted!
"Welcome to the family!" shouted the animals.
And they all shared a big happy hug!

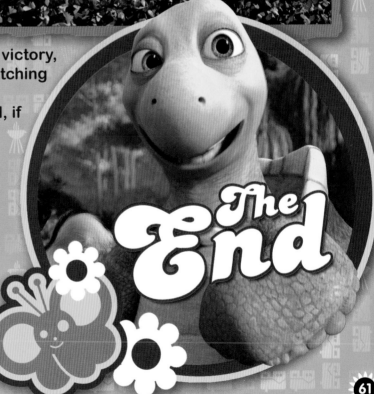

The End

Answers

spot the *P24*
difference!

Ozzie's Wordsearch *P49*

V	F	W	E	R	L	Y	K	I	O
I	H	J	K	P	E	N	N	Y	L
N	G	H	F	D	S	D	A	L	G
C	M	A	B	V	S	C	Z	A	S
E	N	M	Q	W	G	E	R	S	T
N	L	M	P	O	L	I	U	T	Y
T	K	Y	H	E	A	T	H	E	R
J	H	G	F	D	D	S	A	L	A
P	N	M	B	V	Y	C	X	L	S
V	E	R	N	E	S	Y	U	A	I

WE HAVE AN **ANIMAL** PROBLEM.

P36 MASSIVE MUNCHING MAZE

5	4
3	6

R.J has the most food, so he is the winner!